seasons

anne crausaz

Kane Miller
A DIVISION OF EDC PUBLISHING

Everything is green. It must be springtime.

And springtime smells beautiful.

Close your eyes and listen.
The blackbirds are singing about
their favorite season.

If a ladybug lands on you, it might tickle.

It's cherry time.
Are they as sweet as last year's?

Fireflies, like flying stars.
Summer has arrived!

New smells are growing in the vegetable garden: tomato and basil, verbena and mint...

Can you hear that? You're not scared, are you?
It's just a summer storm...

The air is warm, but the water is cold.

Sometimes summer is the taste of sand
in your mouth!

The colors have changed. Autumn is here. The wind is blowing the ants with the seeds. Let's follow them.

Taste the first blackberries,
sweet and sour at the
same time.

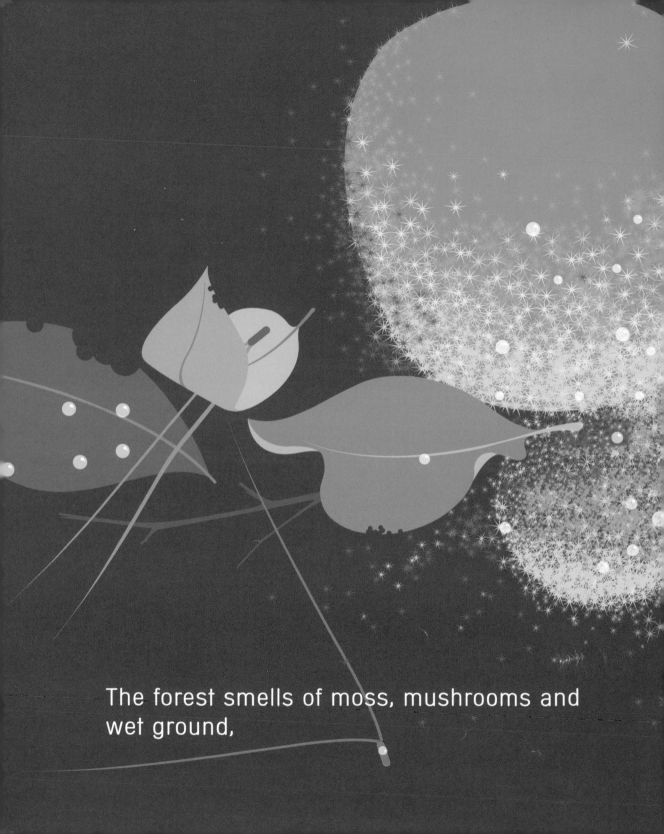

The forest smells of moss, mushrooms and wet ground,

and the leaves make a wonderful crackling sound. Jump in!

The chestnuts are soft, but sticky too.

Now the fog is so thick it's hard to see.
It's winter.

The wood fire smells delicious, and the smoke from the fire looks like it's whispering to the clouds.

Shhhh.   Listen to the silence of the snow.

Cold hands? Don't stay out too long.

Have one last taste of snowflakes.

Because soon, the flowers
will start growing up through
the snow, ready for...